Sleep of Memory

English translations of works by Patrick Modiano

From Yale University Press
After the Circus
Little Jewel
Paris Nocturne
Pedigree: A Memoir
Sleep of Memory
Such Fine Boys
Sundays in August
Suspended Sentences: Three Novellas (Afterimage,
    Suspended Sentences, and Flowers of Ruin)

Also available
The Black Notebook
Catherine Certitude
Dora Bruder
Honeymoon
In the Café of Lost Youth
Lacombe, Lucien
Missing Person
The Occupation Trilogy (The Night Watch, Ring Roads,
    and La Place de l'Etoile)
Out of the Dark
So You Don't Get Lost in the Neighborhood
Villa Triste
Young Once

Sleep of Memory

Patrick Modiano

Translated from the French
by Mark Polizzotti

Yale UNIVERSITY PRESS · NEW HAVEN AND LONDON

A MARGELLOS
WORLD REPUBLIC OF LETTERS BOOK

The Margellos World Republic of Letters is dedicated to making literary works from around the globe available in English through translation. It brings to the English-speaking world the work of leading poets, novelists, essayists, philosophers, and playwrights from Europe, Latin America, Africa, Asia, and the Middle East to stimulate international discourse and creative exchange.

Yale University Press books may be purchased in quantity for educational, business, or promotional use. For information, please e-mail sales.press@yale.edu (U.S. office) or sales@yaleup.co.uk (U.K. office).

Set in MT Baskerville type by Tseng Information Systems, Inc. Printed in the United States of America.

Library of Congress Control Number: 2018937028
ISBN 978-0-300-23830-3 (hardcover : alk. paper)

A catalogue record for this book is available from the British Library.

This paper meets the requirements of ANSI/NISO z39.48-1992 (Permanence of Paper).

10 9 8 7 6 5 4 3 2 1

Sleep of Memory

Once, on the quays, the title of a book caught my eye: *The Time of Encounters*. For me, too, there had been a time of encounters, in a long-distant past. I was prone back then to a fear of nothingness, like a kind of vertigo. I never felt it when alone, only with certain individuals whom I had in fact just encountered. I'd reassure myself that, when the time was right, I could steal away unnoticed. You never knew where some of those people might lead you. It was a slippery slope.

I could start by talking about Sunday evenings. They filled me with dread, as they do anyone who has had to return to boarding school on late winter afternoons, at sunset. That dread pursues them in their dreams, sometimes for the rest of their lives. On Sunday evenings years later, a few people would gather in the apartment of Martine Hayward, and I happened to be among them. I was twenty and felt out of place. Guilt took hold of me again, as if I were still a boarder: as if, instead of going back to school, I had run away.

Must I really start by talking about Martine Hayward and the various individuals surrounding her on those evenings? Or should I follow chronological order? I just don't know.

At around age fourteen, I got used to walking the streets on my own, on my days off from school, after the bus dropped us at Porte d'Orléans. My parents were out, my father absorbed in his deals, my mother acting in a play in Pigalle. That year, 1959, I discovered the Pigalle neighborhood, on Saturday evenings while my mother was onstage, and I often returned there in the decade that followed. I'll provide some more details if I can work up the courage.

At first I was afraid to walk alone, so for reassurance I'd always follow the same path: Rue Fontaine, Place Blanche, Place Pigalle, Rue Frochot, and Rue Victor-Massé up to the bakery on the corner of Rue Pigalle, a curious place that stayed open all night, where I'd buy myself a croissant.

That same winter, on Saturdays when I wasn't at school, I stood watch on Rue Spontini in front of the building where a girl lived whose name I've forgotten, and whom I'll call "Stioppa's daughter." I didn't actually know her. I had gotten her address from Stioppa himself, during one of those walks that he and my father used to take, with me, Sundays in the Bois de Boulogne. Stioppa was Russian, a friend of my father's, and they saw each other frequently. Tall, with dark, oily hair. He used to wear an old overcoat with a fur collar. He'd had some financial setbacks. At around six in the evening, we'd walk him back to the boardinghouse where he lived. He told me he had a daughter my age and that I could call her. Apparently, he no longer saw her, as she lived with her mother and her mother's new husband.

On Saturday afternoons that winter, before going to join my mother in her dressing room at the theater in Pigalle, I would station myself in front of the building on Rue Spontini, waiting for the glass street door with its black ironwork to open and a girl my age, "Stioppa's daughter," to appear. I was certain she would be alone, would walk straight up to me, and it would be perfectly natural to talk with her. But she never came out of the building.

Stioppa had given me her telephone number. Someone picked up. I said, "I'd like to speak with Stioppa's daughter." A pause. I introduced myself as "the son of a friend of Stioppa's." Her voice was clear and warm, as if we were old friends. "Call me next week," she said. "We'll make a date. It's complicated . . . I don't live at my father's . . . I'll explain everything . . ."

But the next week, and all the other weeks that winter, the phone kept ringing without anyone answering. Two or three times, on Saturdays, before taking the metro to Pigalle, I again stood watch in front of the building on Rue Spontini. In vain. I could have rung at the door of their apartment but, as with the telephone, I felt certain no one would answer. And besides, after that spring, there were no more walks in the Bois de Boulogne with Stioppa. Or with my father.

For a long time, I was convinced that the only true encounters were the ones that took place in the street. That's why I waited for Stioppa's daughter on the sidewalk, across from her building, though I had never met her. "I'll explain everything," she had said on the phone. For several days afterward, a voice spoke those words ever more faintly in my dreams. Yes, if I wanted to meet her, it was because I hoped she would give me some "explanations." Perhaps they'd help me understand my father, a stranger who walked next to me in silence, down the paths of the Bois de Boulogne.

She, Stioppa's daughter, and I, Stioppa's friend's son, surely had things in common. And I was certain she knew more about all this than I did.

In that same period, behind the half-open door of his office, my father would speak on the telephone. A phrase of his stuck with me: "the Russian black market crowd." More than forty years later, I came across a list of Russian names, the names of prominent black marketeers in Paris during the German Occupation. Shapochnikov, Kurilo, Stamoglou, Baron Wolf, Mechersky, Djaparidze . . . Was Stioppa's name among them? And my father's, under an assumed Russian identity? I asked myself these questions once more before they became lost, answerless, in the depths of time.

When I was about seventeen, I met a woman, Mireille Ourousov, who also had a Russian name. It was the name of her husband, Eddie Ourousov, aka "the Consul," with whom she lived in Spain, near Torremolinos. She was French, from the Landes region. The dunes, the pine trees, the deserted beaches of the Atlantic, one sundrenched day in September . . . And yet I'd met her in Paris, in the winter of 1962. I had left my boarding school in the Haute-Savoie with a fever of 102, caught the train for Paris, and ended up at around midnight at my mother's apartment. She was away and had given the keys to Mireille Ourousov, who was staying there for a few weeks before heading back to Spain. When I rang at the door, it was she who answered. The apartment looked abandoned. Not a stick of furniture, apart from a folding table and two garden chairs in the foyer, a large bed in the middle of the room that looked out on the river, and in the room next door, where I used to sleep when I was a child, a table, fabric samples, a tailor's dummy, dresses and various garments on hangers. The chandelier gave off a dim light, as most of the bulbs had burned out.

It was a strange February, what with the muted light in the apartment and assassination plots by the paramilitary OAS. Mireille Ourousov was on her way back from a skiing trip and showed me pictures of herself and her friends on the balcony of a chalet. On one of the photos, she was with an actor named Gérard Blain. She told me that Blain, a latchkey child, had started making movies at the age of twelve, without his parents' consent. Later, when I saw him

in a few films, it seemed to me he was always
walking with his hands in his pockets, head
slightly sunken into his shoulders, as if protect-
ing himself from the rain. I spent most of my
days with Mireille Ourousov. Usually we went
out to eat. The gas in the apartment had been
cut and we had to cook on an alcohol burner.
No heat. But there were still a few logs left in
the bedroom fireplace. One morning, we went
to an office near Odéon to pay off a two-month-
overdue electricity bill: for a while, we wouldn't
have to light our way by candle. Almost every
night, at around midnight, she would take me
to a cabaret on Rue des Saints-Pères, right near
the apartment, long after the show was over. At
the bar on the ground floor there were still a few
patrons, who all seemed to know one another
and spoke in low voices. We joined up with a
friend of hers, one Jacques de Bavière (or Deba-
vière), an athletic-looking blond; she said he was
a "journalist" who "shuttled back and forth between Paris and Algiers." I suppose that when
she sometimes stayed out all night, it was to

meet up with this Jacques de Bavière (or Deba-
vière), who lived in a studio on Avenue Paul-
Doumer. I went there with her one afternoon
because she'd left her watch. Jacques de Bavière
was out. He had taken us a few times to a restaurant off the Champs-Elysées, on Rue Washing-
ton, the Rose des Sables. Much later, I learned
that the cabaret on Rue des Saints-Pères and
the Rose des Sables were frequented at the time
by members of a parapolice group involved in
the Algerian War. And given the coincidence, I
wondered whether Jacques de Bavière (or Deba-
vière) might have been part of that organization.
Another winter, in the seventies, at around six
in the evening as I was going into the George-V
metro stop, I saw coming out a man who might
have been a slightly older Jacques de Bavière.
I made an about-face and followed him, thinking I should go up to him to ask what had become of Mireille Ourousov. Was she still living
in Torremolinos with her husband, Eddie, "the
Consul"? He walked toward the Rond-Point
des Champs-Elysées, limping slightly. I stopped

when I reached the Café Marignan and gazed after him until he became lost in the crowd. Why hadn't I approached him? Would he have recognized me? I can't answer those questions. For me, Paris is littered with ghosts, as numerous as metro stations and all the dots that light up when you press the buttons on the electric route map.

We often took the metro, Mireille Ourousov and I, at the Louvre station, to go to the neighborhoods in the west of Paris, where she visited friends whose faces I've forgotten. What remains clear in my memory is crossing the Seine with her over the Pont des Arts, then the square in front of the church of Saint-Germain-l'Auxerrois, and sometimes the courtyard of the Louvre with, way in back, the yellow light of the police outpost, the same muted light as in the apartment. There were books on the shelves in my former room, near the large window on the right, and today I wonder by what miracle they had remained there, forgotten, when everything else had vanished. Books my mother read when she'd arrived in Paris in 1942—novels by

Hans Fallada, books in Flemish—and also books for young readers that had belonged to me: *The Mystery Freighter* and *The Vicomte of Bragelonne* . . .

Down in the Haute-Savoie, they had finally gotten concerned about my absence. One morning the telephone rang, and Mireille Ourousov answered. Father Janin, the school principal, wanted to know what had become of me, as they'd had no word for two weeks.

She told him I was "not feeling well"—a bad cold—and that she'd let him know the exact date when I "planned to return." I asked her point-blank: Could I go with her to Spain? As a minor, I would need written authorization from my parents to cross the border. And the fact that I hadn't yet reached adulthood suddenly seemed of great concern to Mireille Ourousov, so much so that she resolved to ask Jacques de Bavière's advice on the matter.

My favorite time of day in Paris in winter was morning, between six o'clock and eight-thirty, when it was still dark out. A respite before daybreak. Time was suspended and you felt lighter than usual.

I frequented various cafés at the hour when they opened their doors to the first customers. In the winter of 1964, in one of those dawn cafés— as I called them—when any hope seemed warranted as long as it was still dark, I would meet up with a certain Geneviève Dalame.

The café was on the ground floor of one of those squat buildings, toward the end of Boule-

vard de la Gare in the 13th arrondissement.
Today, the boulevard has been renamed and
the squat houses and buildings, on the odd-
numbered side before Place d'Italie, have been
torn down. Sometimes I seem to recall the café
was named the Bar Vert; at other times this
memory fades, like words you've just heard in a
dream that elude you when you wake.

Geneviève Dalame was always the first to ar-
rive, and when I entered the café I would see
her sitting at the same table, way in back, head
bowed over an open book. She'd told me she
slept barely four hours a night. She worked as a
secretary at Polydor Studios, a bit farther down
the boulevard, which was why we would meet
in that café before she went to work. I had gotten to know her in an occult bookstore on Rue
Geoffroy-Saint-Hilaire. She was very interested
in the occult. I was too. Not that I wanted to
submit to a doctrine or become some guru's disciple, but because I liked mystery.

When we left the bookstore, it was after sunset. And at that hour, in winter, I had the same

feeling of lightness as very early in the morning, when it was still dark. From then on, the 5th arrondissement, with its many neighborhoods and its far reaches toward Boulevard de la Gare, would remain associated for me with Geneviève Dalame.

At around eight-thirty, we would walk to her office along the median strip, where the elevated train ran overhead. I asked her about Polydor Studios. I had just passed an entrance exam to become a "lyricist" at the Composers' and Music Publishers' Guild, and I needed a "sponsor" in order to enroll. A certain Emil Stern, a songwriter, bandleader, and pianist, had agreed to sponsor me. He had conducted the orchestra for Edith Piaf's first recordings, twenty-five years earlier, at Polydor Studios. I asked Geneviève Dalame if the studio archives still held any trace of that. One morning, at the café, she handed me an envelope containing the old log sheets for Edith Piaf's recording sessions, conducted by my "sponsor," Emil Stern. She seemed rather embarrassed at having stolen those files for me.

At first, she hesitated to tell me where she lived, exactly. When I asked, she answered, "In a hotel." We'd known each other for two weeks, and one evening, when I'd given her a copy of the *Practical Dictionary of the Occult Sciences* by Marianne Verneuil and a novel having to do with esotericism, *In Memory of an Angel,* she asked me to escort her back to that hotel.

It was located at the bottom of Rue Monge, at the fringes of Les Gobelins and the 13th arrondissement. Nearly half a century has passed and people no longer live in hotel rooms in Paris, as was often the case after the war and into the 1960s. Geneviève Dalame was the last person I knew who lived in a hotel. It also seems to me that in those years, 1963, 1964, the old world took one last breath before collapsing, like all those houses and apartment buildings on the outskirts that they were about to demolish. We were given the opportunity, we who were very young, to live for a few final months in those ancient surroundings. At the hotel on Rue Monge, I remember the pear-shaped light switch on the

nightstand, and the black drapes that Geneviève Dalame always pulled shut with a sharp
tug, drapes from the time of "passive defense,"
which they hadn't changed since the war.

She introduced me to her brother a few weeks after we'd met, a brother she had never mentioned before. Once or twice I'd tried to find out more about her family, but I could tell she was reluctant to answer and I didn't insist.

One morning, I entered the café on Boulevard de la Gare and found her sitting at the usual table across from a dark-haired boy about our age. I sat on the bench, next to her. He was wearing a zipped jacket with padded shoulders, which seemed to be made of leopard skin. He smiled at me and ordered a grog in a ringing voice, as if he were a regular customer.

Geneviève Dalame said, "This is my brother," and from her discomfited expression I understood that he had shown up unexpectedly.

He asked me "what I did in life," and I answered evasively. Then, as if this bit of information could be useful to him, he asked a question that surprised me: "You live in Paris?" I thought to myself that *he* hadn't always lived in Paris. Geneviève Dalame had told me she was born in the Vosges, though I don't remember whether it was in Epinal or Saint-Dié. I could easily imagine her brother at a café table in one of those two cities at around 11 P.M., a café near the train station, the only one still open. He would no doubt be wearing the same ill-fitting jacket, in fake leopard skin; and that jacket, entirely unremarkable in a Paris street, would have attracted plenty of notice down there. He would be sitting alone, gaze unfocused, in front of a pint, while the last game of pool was being played.

He wanted to accompany Geneviève Dalame

to her office, and we walked along the median strip of the boulevard. She looked increasingly uncomfortable in his presence, as if she wanted to get rid of him. My impression was confirmed when he asked whether she still lived in that same hotel on Rue Monge. "I'm moving out next week," she told him. "I've found another place, near Auteuil." He kept asking for the address. She gave him a number on Rue Michel-Ange, as if she'd been expecting the question. From the inner pocket of his jacket he took a black leather address book and jotted down the information. Then she left us at the door of Poly-dor Studios, telling me, "See you later," with a slight nod of complicity.

I found myself alone with that fellow in the leopard-skin jacket. "What say we go have a drink?" he asked in a peremptory tone. Snow had begun falling in heavy wet flakes, almost like raindrops. "I don't have time," I told him. "I have to meet someone." But he kept walking beside me, and I was tempted to shake him by running to the nearest metro stop, Chevaleret, a few hundred yards away. "Have you known Geneviève very long? Doesn't she get on your nerves with all that crap about magic and séance tables?" "Not at all." He asked if I lived in the neighborhood, and I was certain he'd try to find out my address so he could enter it in his little black book. "I live outside the city," I said. And I felt a bit ashamed of that lie. "In Saint-Cloud." He took out his black book. I had to invent an address, an avenue with a name like Anatole-France or Romain-Rolland. "And do you have a phone?" I hesitated a moment on the exchange, then came up with "Val-d'Or," followed by four digits. He wrote it down carefully. "I want to enroll in an acting class. Do you know of any?" He gave me an insistent stare. "People tell me I've got the look." He was tall, with fairly regular features and curly black hair. "You know," I replied, "in Paris, there are bucketloads of acting classes." He seemed taken aback, no doubt because of the expression "bucketloads." He zipped his fake-leopard-skin jacket to his chin and turned up his collar against the snow, which was falling more heavily. I had finally reached the subway entrance. I was afraid he'd follow me and I'd never lose him. I went down the steps without saying good-bye or turning around, and I snuck onto the station platform just as the barrier swung shut behind me.

Geneviève Dalame wasn't surprised by how I had acted around her brother. After all, hadn't she herself given him a false hotel address? She told me he'd come to the café to ask her for money. Naturally, he knew the café where we met early in the morning and where she worked, but she said it wasn't hard to get rid of people. I couldn't share her optimism. She added, in a very calm voice, that her brother would end up going back to the Vosges and living off "petty schemes"—that was the expression she used—as he'd always done. Days went by without our seeing hide or hair of him. Perhaps he really had gone back to the Vosges.

For a time, I pictured this brother of Geneviève Dalame's going into a phone booth and dialing the Val-d'Or number, which no one would answer. Or else, he would hear, "You have the wrong number, sir," the sentence falling like a guillotine blade. And I imagined him taking the metro and crossing the Seine into Saint-Cloud, dressed in his fake-leopard-skin jacket. The winter that year was especially harsh, as he, collar turned up, went looking for an avenue that didn't exist. For all eternity.

Geneviève Dalame regularly went to visit a woman whom she considered a friend, and who, according to her, was well versed in the occult. She had told her about our meeting and that I had given her Marianne Verneuil's *Dictionary* and the novel *In Memory of an Angel*. One day, she asked me to come with her to see this Madeleine Péraud, whose name I've had a hard time recalling. But with a little effort they come back to you, those names that lie dormant beneath a thin coating of snow and neglect. Yes, Madeleine Péraud. But I might be wrong about her first name.

She lived near the start of Rue du Val-de-Grâce, at number 9. Since then, I've often passed by its gate, which led to a garden surrounded on three sides by building façades with large windows. I even found myself there, by chance, about two weeks ago, around the same time of day as when Geneviève Dalame and I would pass through that gate. Five o'clock on a winter evening, as darkness was falling and lights were already appearing in the windows. I felt as if I'd gone back into the past by a phenomenon we could call *eternal return;* or else it simply meant that, for me, time had stopped at a given period in my life.

Madeleine Péraud was a brunette of around forty, with hair in a bun, pale eyes, and the gait and bearing of an ex-dancer. How had Geneviève Dalame met her? I believe she had first gone to see her for yoga lessons, but I also seem to recall that before introducing us, Geneviève Dalame spoke of her as "Doctor Péraud." Did she practice medicine? This all happened a good fifty years ago, and I have to admit that during that half-century I haven't thought much about all those people I came across. Brief encounters.

After Geneviève Dalame introduced us, I accompanied her several times to Madeleine Péraud's at five in the evening—always on a Thursday. She led us in silence down a hallway and into the salon. The two tall windows looked out onto the garden and we sat down: Geneviève Dalame and I on the red sofa, facing the windows; Madeleine Péraud on a cushion, legs folded, back very straight. At our first meeting, she asked me in her deep, husky voice whether I was a student, and I told her the truth: "No, I'm not studying." I had enrolled at the Sorbonne just to extend my military deferment, but I never went to class. I was a phantom student. She wanted to know whether I had a job, and I said I more or less supported myself by working for various booksellers, as what we might call, though I didn't like the trade term very much, a "book dealer." And I had joined the Composers' and Music Publishers' Guild in hopes of writing song lyrics. That was all. "And what

about your parents?" I suddenly realized that at
my age, I could have had parents who offered
me moral, emotional, or financial support. But
no, no parents. And my answer was so laconic
that she didn't ask anything further about my
family. It was the first time I'd given such spon-
taneous answers to questions about my life.
Until then, I had always avoided them, as I felt
a natural distrust toward any form of interroga-
tion. Perhaps I'd relaxed that evening because of
Madeleine Péraud's gaze and voice, which con-
veyed a sort of tranquility, the sense that someone was listening, which I wasn't used to. She
asked good questions, the way an acupuncturist
knows exactly where to place his needles. And
besides, hadn't Geneviève Dalame, more than
once, called her "Doctor Péraud"? And there
was also the quiet of the salon, the two tall windows facing out onto the garden, the light from
the floor lamp between the windows, which left
areas of shadow. The silence made you wonder
whether you were really in Paris. I spent most
of my days outside, in the streets and in pub-

lic places, cafés, the metro, hotel rooms, movie houses. And "Doctor Péraud's" apartment stood in contrast to all that, especially in winter, the winters of the early sixties, which I remember as being much harsher than winters today. I admit that on my first visit to "Doctor Péraud," I thought how comforting it would be to take shelter from the winter cold in her apartment, and to answer the questions she would ask me in that voice of hers, so deep and calm.

At Madeleine Péraud's, I took the liberty of looking through the volumes in a low bookcase, at the back of the salon. I told her I didn't mean to be nosy; it was just out of "professional" curiosity. "If you find any books that interest you, take them." She encouraged me with a smile. They were mostly titles devoted to the occult sciences—among them, the one I had given Geneviève Dalame, which had been published about ten years before: *In Memory of an Angel.* "I was surprised you knew of that novel," said Madeleine Péraud, as if this book reminded her of something in particular: more than just literary, something personal.

I had pulled it from the shelf and opened it mechanically. On the half-title page, a dedication in large handwriting in blue ink: "For you. A souvenir of the angels. Megève. Le Mauvais Pas. Irène." She noticed that I'd read the inscription and seemed embarrassed. "A lovely novel," she said. "But I have other books for the two of you to read," she added in an authoritarian tone. One evening, she placed on the red sofa between Geneviève Dalame and me a volume called *Meetings with Remarkable Men*. Today, fifty years later, that title and the word "meetings" make me think of something that had never occurred to me: Unlike many people my age, I never tried to meet the four or five intellectual guides who dominated university life in those days, or become their disciple. Why? In my capacity as an absentee student, it would have been natural for me to seek out a mentor, living as I did in a state of solitude and confusion. I remember only one of those guides, and that was because I ran into him, very late one night, on Rue du Colisée: I would have expected to see him instead near the major universities. That night, I was struck by his stumbling gait, the sadness and anxiety in his eyes. He seemed lost. I took him by the arm and led him, at his request, to the nearest taxi stand.

I had guessed early on that "Doctor Péraud" wielded some influence over Geneviève Dalame. One evening as we were leaving her place, after crossing the garden, she told me that Madeleine Péraud belonged to a "group"—a kind of secret society—where they practiced "magic." She couldn't tell me any more, as she didn't understand much about it herself. Madeleine Péraud would allude to this group, but always in vague terms, no doubt to observe Geneviève Dalame's reaction, before getting down to business. Still, it seemed to me that Geneviève Dalame knew more about this than she let on, especially when she blurted out: "You could talk to her about it." We were skirting the garden wall, before the church of Saint-Jacques du Haut-Pas. "Yes, you should talk to her about it." I was surprised at

her insistence. "Have you known her very long?"
I asked. "Not very long. I met her one afternoon,
in a café, near where she lives, across from the
Val-de-Grâce." She seemed about to provide
other details, but then she fell silent. We came
out onto that very wide street that borders the
modern buildings of the Ecole Normale Supé-
rieure and the Ecole de Physique et Chimie,
which make you feel like you've wandered by
mistake into a foreign city—Berlin, Lausanne,
or even Rome, in the Parioli neighborhood—
so much so that you begin to wonder if you're
walking in a dream, and you end up doubting
your own identity. "You really should talk to
her about it," Geneviève Dalame repeated. Her
voice sounded anxious, as if she were sending me
a call for help. "She'll bring you up to speed . . ."
I was about to ask, "Up to speed about what?"
but I sensed that such a direct question would
only heighten her discomfort and that she really
was under the sway of "Doctor Péraud." "Yes,
of course I'll talk to her," and I labored to affect
a calm, detached tone. "Next Thursday, when

we go see her. I'm intrigued by that woman. She seems very smart. I'd like to know more about her."

We had reached the entrance to her hotel. She looked relieved. She gave me a smile. I believe she was grateful for my apparent eagerness to learn more. I had truly meant what I said. Ever since my childhood and adolescence, I'd felt a lively curiosity and a particular attraction for anything related to the mysteries of Paris.

B ut I didn't wait for the following Thursday to "know more." One morning, after I'd accompanied Geneviève Dalame from her hotel to Polydor Studios, I took the metro in the opposite direction and, exiting at Censier-Daubenton, headed to the Val-de-Grâce.

I arrived at the gate and walked across the garden without breaking stride. As I was passing through the main door to the building, it occurred to me that I should have phoned Madeleine Péraud to ask whether she was available.

I was surprised by the sound of her doorbell, which I hadn't noticed when I was on that landing with Geneviève Dalame: spindly, muted notes that sounded like they might die out at any second. I kept my finger on the button, not sure that Madeleine Péraud could hear the ring if she happened to be in the back room.

The door opened partway without my having heard the slightest sound of steps. Did she camp out behind it, waiting for possible visitors? She didn't seem surprised to see me. As always, she led me in silence down the hallway. It was the first time I'd been in that salon in daytime. Sunlight dappled the parquet floor. Through the window, I could see the garden under a thin coating of snow. I felt even farther from Paris than on the evenings when I came here with Geneviève Dalame.

She sat on my left on the red sofa, in the spot usually occupied by Geneviève Dalame. She stared at me.

"Geneviève just called to say you wanted to see me. I was expecting you."

So this visit had been planned behind my

back. Perhaps the two of them had hypnotized me without my knowing it.

"She called?"

I felt as if I'd already lived through this scene in a dream. A ray of sunlight hit the bookcase on the back wall. There was a moment of silence. It was my turn to break it.

"I read the book you lent me . . . *Meetings with Remarkable Men* . . . I'd already heard of it . . ."

One of my classmates at boarding school in the Haute-Savoie, Pierre Andrieux, had told me that his parents were disciples of the book's author, George Ivanòvich Gurdjieff, a "spiritual teacher." On one of our days off, Pierre Andrieux's mother had driven us to the Plateau d'Assy to visit a woman she was friends with, a pharmacist and another follower of this Gurdjieff. I had overheard bits of their conversation. It was about the "groups" that this man had created around himself, the better to disseminate his "teaching." And the term *groups* had piqued my interest.

"Is that so? You'd heard of it? In what circumstances?"

Her expression was at once worried and interested, as if she feared I might be privy to certain secrets.

"I spent a lot of time in the Haute-Savoie. There were several disciples of George Ivanovich Gurdjieff . . ."

I had said this slowly, holding her gaze.

"In the Haute-Savoie?"

Apparently, she wasn't expecting me to provide this detail. It was as if I were a cop who tries to obtain a confession through surprise. But I wasn't a cop. At most a nice young man.

"Yes . . . in the Haute-Savoie . . . near the Plateau d'Assy . . . not far from Megève . . ."

I remembered the inscription on the novel *In Memory of an Angel* that was surely meant for her. "For you . . . Megève . . . Le Mauvais Pas . . ."

"And you met some disciples of Gurdjieff . . . in the Haute-Savoie?"

"Yes, a few."

I had the impression she was waiting nervously for me to name names.

"The mother of one of my classmates at school . . . She brought us to see a friend of hers who was also a follower of Gurdjieff . . . a pharmacist . . . in the Plateau d'Assy."

I read the astonishment on her face.

"But I knew her, a long time ago . . . I knew that pharmacist in the Plateau d'Assy . . . She was also called Geneviève — Geneviève Lief . . ."

"I never knew her name," I said.

She tilted her head as if trying to remember the woman more clearly. And perhaps to recall other details of that time in her life.

"I went to see her several times, in the Plateau d'Assy . . ."

She had forgotten my presence. I kept silent, not wanting to distract her from her thoughts. After a moment, she turned to face me.

"I would never have expected you to remind me of all these things."

She appeared so unsettled that I wondered whether I shouldn't change the subject.

"Geneviève said you give yoga lessons. I'd like very much to study yoga with you."

She hadn't heard me. Her head tilted once more; she was no doubt trying to regroup her few remaining memories of that pharmacist from the Plateau d'Assy.

She leaned closer to me. Our faces were almost touching. She said in a murmur:

"I was very young . . . I must have been your age . . . I had a friend named Irène . . . She was the one who brought me to the meetings at Gurdjieff's, in Paris, on Rue des Colonels-Renard . . . There was a whole group of disciples around him . . ."

She spoke rapidly, in staccato, as if talking to a confessor. I felt a little embarrassed. I was neither old enough nor experienced enough to play the role of confessor.

"And then I left with my friend Irène for the Haute-Savoie, to Megève and the Plateau d'Assy . . . She needed treatment in a sanatorium in the Plateau d'Assy . . ."

She was ready to tell me her life story. All

kinds of people have done so in the years since, and I've often wondered why. I must inspire trust. I like to listen to people and ask questions. I often happened to catch bits of strangers' conversations in cafés. I would jot them down as discreetly as possible. At least those words wouldn't be lost forever. They fill five notebooks, replete with dates and ellipses.

"Is Irène the one who inscribed *In Memory of an Angel* to you?" I asked.

"That's right."

"At the end of the inscription, she wrote 'Le Mauvais Pas.' I know the Mauvais Pas."

She knit her brow and looked as if she were searching her memory.

"It was a kind of nightclub where I used to go with Irène."

I hadn't forgotten that derelict building on the road to Mont d'Arbois, part of which bore traces of a fire. On its façade hung a sign in light-colored wood, with, in red letters, the words "Mauvais Pas"—the "Tight Spot." I had spent several months in a children's home, a few hundred yards from there and a bit farther up.

"I haven't been back to the Haute-Savoie since then," she said brusquely, as if to cut short our conversation.

"After you met Gurdjieff, were you in the 'groups'?"

She seemed taken aback by the question.

"I'm asking because my friend's mother and the pharmacist from the Plateau d'Assy often used that word . . ."

"It was Gurdjieff's word," she answered. "He talked about 'work groups' and 'working on oneself' . . ."

But I don't think she wanted to give me any more particulars about the doctrine of George Ivanovich Gurdjieff.

"Your friend Geneviève," she suddenly said. "It's crazy how much she looks like Irène . . . The first time I saw her in that café, across from the Val-de-Grâce, it was a shock. I thought it *was* Irène . . ."

I wasn't at all troubled by what she had just confided. Since my childhood, I had overheard so many strange things through half-open doors or thin hotel walls, in cafés and waiting rooms and overnight trains . . .

"I'm very concerned about Geneviève . . . That's what I wanted to talk to you about."

"Concerned? How so?"

"She's got a strange way of living, as if, now and then, she simply removes herself from life . . . Don't you think?"

"No."

"It's odd that you don't see it . . . She sometimes looks like she's walking around with her head in the clouds. Haven't you ever noticed? Doesn't she ever remind you of a somnambulist?"

The word called to mind the title of a ballet I'd seen as a child, which had left a fond memory. I tried to think what similarity might exist between Geneviève Dalame and that ballerina slowly climbing the stairs, arms outstretched.

"A somnambulist . . . You could be right," I said.

I didn't want to antagonize her.

"Irène was exactly like her . . . exactly . . . She had moments of complete absence . . . I tried to fight against that."

"And what did Gurdjieff make of this?"

I immediately regretted asking. Back then, I was prone to blurting out inappropriate questions. I wanted to have done with it. From listening to so many people and paying them such close attention, I sometimes experienced an abrupt feeling of weariness and a sudden desire to cut all ties.

"Gurdjieff was a good influence on her. On me as well. I always encouraged Irène to follow his teachings."

She turned toward me and stared at me pointedly. It was unnerving.

"We must help Geneviève."

Her tone was so serious that she ended up convincing me Geneviève Dalame was in imminent danger. And yet, as much as I thought about it, I couldn't imagine what sort of danger that might be.

"You have to persuade her to come live here."

I was amazed that she would give me such a mission.

"It's very bad for Geneviève to live in a hotel. Irène was exactly like her. I know the problem all too well . . . I spent three months telling her to leave that horrible hotel on Rue d'Armaillé. Luckily the meetings at Gurdjieff's took place in that same neighborhood, otherwise Irène would never have left her room . . ."

Clearly, this Irène had meant a lot to her.

"The hotel she was living in was right near Gurdjieff's?" I asked.

"Just a stone's throw . . . Irène had taken a room there in order to be as close to Gurdjieff's as possible."

And so, you need only come across a person, or meet him two or three times, or hear him say something in a café or train corridor, to pick up snatches of his life. My notebooks are filled with bits of sentences spoken by anonymous voices. And today, on a page no different from the others, I try to transcribe the few words exchanged nearly fifty years ago with a certain Madeleine Péraud, whose first name I'm not even sure of. Irène, the Plateau d'Assy, Gurdjieff, a hotel on Rue d'Armaillé . . .

"You have to persuade Geneviève to come live here."

Once more, she spoke in a murmur and had moved her face close to mine. She looked me right in the eye, and her gaze made me feel paralyzed, as in those dreams when you try to flee but are rooted to the spot.

A rather long time must have passed, several hours that I can't recall, a memory lapse. Night was falling, the salon was in shadow, and I was still on the red sofa with her.

She stood up and went to turn on the floor lamp between the two windows. She walked to the bookcase and picked out two items from the shelves.

"Here . . . you can have more whenever you like . . ."

The two books were thin, almost like pamphlets: Suzuki's *Essays in Zen Buddhism*, second series, and *The Sacred Rite of Magical Love* by Maria de Naglowska. I still have them fifty years later, and I wonder why some books or objects persist in following you around your whole life, without your knowledge, while others, much more precious, are lost.

In the entryway, I was about to open the apartment door to leave when she laid her hand on my arm.

"Are you heading off to see Geneviève?"

I felt embarrassed about answering, so badly did she seem to envy me.

"I meant to tell you . . . you could live here, with her . . . I would be very happy to take you in . . ."

Six years later, I was walking along Rue Geoffroy-Saint-Hilaire, near the Mosque and the wall surrounding the botanical gardens. A woman was walking ahead of me, holding a little boy by the hand. Her nonchalant gait reminded me of someone. I couldn't help staring at her.

I quickened my pace and caught up to the woman and little boy. I turned toward her. Geneviève Dalame. We hadn't seen each other in those six years. She smiled at me as if we'd just parted company the day before.

"Do you live in this neighborhood?"

I was using the formal *vous*, but I don't know why. Probably because of the little boy's presence. Yes, she lived right nearby. I tried to make conversation, but she seemed to find it perfectly natural that we should walk next to each other in silence.

We entered the botanical gardens and followed a path to the zoo. The little boy ran ahead of us, then turned around and ran back, pretending to escape from invisible pursuers; sometimes he ducked behind a tree trunk. I asked if he was her son. Yes. Was she married? No. She lived alone with her boy. In short, we had found each other again six years later in the same street where we'd first met, but it didn't seem as if any time had passed. On the contrary, it had stopped, and our first encounter was recurring, with a variation: the presence of that child. And we would meet yet again, in that same street, as the hands of a watch come together every day at noon and midnight. Moreover, on the evening when I'd met her for the first time, at the occult bookstore on Rue Geoffroy-Saint-Hilaire, I had bought a book whose title had struck me: *The Eternal Return of the Same.*

We had arrived at the cages of the zoo, empty that day save for the largest one, in which they'd shut a panther. The little boy had stopped and watched it through the bars. Geneviève Dalame and I had taken seats on a bench, farther back.

"I bring him here to see the animals because of *The Jungle Book.* He wants me to read it to him every night."

I then recalled the few bookshelves near the large window in my mother's empty apartment on the quays. I was certain that alongside the Hans Fallada novels and *The Vicomte of Bragelonne* there were still the two volumes of *The Jungle Book,* in an illustrated edition. I would have to work up the nerve to go back there, to verify that I wasn't mistaken.

I hesitated to mention her sudden disappearance. One evening, at the hotel on Rue Monge, they had told me she'd checked out "permanently." The next day, at Polydor Studios, one of her colleagues had said curtly that she was "on leave," without providing further details. At Madeleine Péraud's, on Rue du Val-de-Grâce, no one answered the door. And I, having gotten used to disappearances since childhood, hadn't really been surprised by Geneviève Dalame's.

"So, you took off without leaving a forwarding address?" She shrugged. But I didn't need any explanations. The little boy came up to us and announced that he was going to open the cage door and walk around with the panther, which he called Bagheera, the panther from *The Jungle Book*. Then he took up position again in front of the bars, waiting for Bagheera to come closer.

"Have you had any word from Doctor Péraud?"

In a detached tone, as if speaking of a vague acquaintance, she explained that Doctor Péraud no longer lived on Rue du Val-de-Grâce, but in the 15th arrondissement. Those people you often wonder about, whose disappearance is shrouded in mystery, a mystery you'll never be able to solve — you'd be surprised to learn that they simply changed neighborhoods.

"And you're not working for Polydor Studios anymore?" No, she still worked there. But like Madeleine Péraud, they were no longer at the same address. From Boulevard de la Gare, Polydor Studios had found a home near Place de Clichy.

I again thought of those electric maps near the ticket windows in the metro. Every station had its corresponding button on the keyboard. And you had only to press the button to see where you needed to transfer. The routes appeared on the map in lines of different-colored lights. I was sure that, in the future, you'd need only enter onto a screen the name of a person you had met once upon a time and a red dot would indicate the spot in Paris where you could find them.

"I ran into your brother once," I told her. She'd had no word from him since that morning when he'd come to ask for money. And when had I run into him? Two or three years ago. I was walking down Boulevard Saint-Michel and was going past La Source, a large café that I had always hesitated to enter without quite knowing why. I recognized him right off the bat because of his fake-leopard-skin jacket. He was sitting at a table next to the glass façade, with a fellow his age. He had stood up and banged on the glass with both fists to get my attention. He was about to join me on the sidewalk, but I beat him to it and pushed open the door to the café, as one confronts a perilous situation in a dream, with the certainty that one could wake up at any moment. I sat down at their table. The discomfort I felt every time I walked by La Source became sharper: I felt as if everyone in the place was under threat of a police raid.

From his jacket pocket he drew his black notebook and, after looking in it, smiled at me sarcastically.

"I tried calling you at Val-d'Or 1414 a few years ago, but evidently you were out."

I sat there, facing him, in the hopes that he'd

tell me something about Geneviève Dalame, perhaps the reasons for her disappearance.

He introduced his friend. His name, Alain Parquenne, has stuck in my memory because I read it ten years later on Avenue de Wagram, on the sign of a tiny shop selling used cameras that he was surely fencing. I'd been tempted to go inside to remember myself to that ghost.

"Geneviève? Haven't you seen her these past three years? Neither have I . . . She must be deep into her tarot cards and crystal balls, as usual . . ."

His fake-leopard-skin jacket looked even rattier than when we'd first met. I noticed a rip at one of the wrists and a stain on his sleeve. As for Alain Parquenne, he had pasty skin and the face of a prematurely aged child—the face of a former stable boy or jockey.

"He's a photographer," Geneviève Dalame's brother told me. "He's making me a press book that I can show agents. I want to break into the movies . . ."

The other watched me while smoking a cigarette, and his glutinous black eyes disturbed me. Abruptly, Geneviève Dalame's brother said to him, "Time for you to call and let them know." Alain Parquenne stood up and headed toward the back of the room.

"I'm sure you could help me out," Geneviève Dalame's brother said to me, with a fixed stare that sent a chill up my spine, the greedy look of someone who would rob corpses after a bombardment.

"Don't you want to help me?" His features had tensed and betrayed a certain bitterness. The other reappeared at our table.

"So, did you let them know?" asked Geneviève Dalame's brother. The other nodded and sat down. I was seized by a wave of panic that I had a hard time getting under control. Who were those people he'd called? Let them know what? I felt as if I were suddenly caught in a mousetrap and the police would bust in at any moment.

"I asked if he'll help us out," he said, pointing at me.

"Yeah, you have to give us a hand," the other said with an evil smile. "Anyway, we're not letting you go . . ."

I stood up and moved toward the café exit. Geneviève Dalame's brother came after me and blocked my path. The other one moved in close behind me, as if he wanted to keep me from turning back. I thought: I have to get out of here before the police bust in. And with a sharp jab of the knee and shoulder, I shoved Geneviève Dalame's brother aside. Then I rammed my fist into the other's face. I was finally in the open air, free. I ran down the boulevard. They both ran after me. I managed to lose them near the Café de Cluny.

"You should never have talked to my brother. As far as I'm concerned, he's dead. He's capable of anything. He's already done time in Epinal."

She had spoken these words in a very low voice, as if she didn't want the little boy to hear, though he was still standing in front of the cage bars, watching the panther.

"What's his name?" I asked.

"Pierre."

It was my chance to discover what her life had been like those past six years. Today, February 1, 2017, I regret not having asked specific questions. But at the time, I was sure she'd answer evasively, or not at all. "She walks around with her head in the clouds," Madeleine Péraud had once said to me. And she had used the word "somnambulist." It reminded me of the ballet I'd seen as a child, featuring a dancer whose name I still recall: Maria Tallchief. Maybe Geneviève Dalame walked "with her head in the clouds," but her step was light and supple, like a dancer's.

"Has he started school yet?" I asked, looking at Pierre.

"His school is across the botanical gardens."

There was no point talking to her about the past. If I had alluded to certain details from six years ago — the café on Boulevard de la Gare, the hotel on Rue Monge, the few people that "Doctor Péraud" had introduced to us, the rather dubious circumstances that she'd dragged us into—she would have been very surprised. She had surely forgotten all of it. Or else, she saw it all from a great distance—greater and greater as the years progressed. And the landscape became lost in fog. She lived in the present.

"Do you have time to walk us home?" she asked.

She took Pierre by the hand, and he looked back to glance one last time at the bars of the cage, behind which Bagheera turned in endless circles.

We walked past the occult bookstore where we had first met. A sign said that it would re-open at two o'clock. We looked at the volumes displayed in the window: *Powers from Within, The Masters and the Path, The Adventurers of Mystery* . . .

"Maybe we could come here tonight to look for some books," I proposed to Geneviève Dalame. Rendezvous at six o'clock, the same time as six years before. It was in this bookstore, after all, that I'd found the volume that had given me so much to ponder: *The Eternal Re-*

turn of the Same. At every page, I said to myself: If we could relive something we'd already experienced, in the same time, the same place, and the same circumstances, but live it much better than the first time, without the mistakes, hitches, and idle moments, it would be like making a clean copy of a heavily revised manuscript . . . The three of us had arrived at an area that I had often walked through with her, between Rue Monge, the Mosque, and Rue du Puits-de-l'Ermite.

She stopped in front of a building that was larger than the others and had balconies. "This is where I live." Pierre opened the street door by himself. I followed them in. I had the feeling I'd already come here in some former life to visit someone. "Tonight at six, at the bookstore," Geneviève Dalame said. "And after, we can have dinner here . . ."

They left me in the entryway. I stood at the foot of the stairs. Now and then, Pierre leaned his head over the ramp, as if he wanted to make sure I was still there. And each time, I waved at him. Then he stood there watching me, chin resting on the banister, while Geneviève Dalame must have been unlocking the door to the apartment. I heard the door shut behind them and felt a pang. But leaving the building, I couldn't see any reason to be sad. For a few months more or, who knows, a few years, despite time's fugitive passing and the successive disappearances of people and things, there was a fixed point: Geneviève Dalame. Pierre. Rue de Quatrefages. Number 5.

I'm trying to impose some order on my memories. Every one of them is a piece of the puzzle, but many are missing, and most of them remain isolated. Sometimes I manage to connect three or four, but no more than that. So I jot down bits and pieces that come back to me in no particular order, lists of names or brief phrases. I hope that these names, like magnets, will draw others to the surface, and that those bits of sentences might end up forming paragraphs and chapters that link together. Meanwhile, I spend my days in a large shed that looks like an old auto repair shop, in search of lost people and objects.

Djorie Bruss

Emmanuel Brucken (photographer)

Jean Meyer (Blue-Eyed Jean)

Gaelle and Guy Vincent

Annie Caisley, 11 Rue des Marronniers

Van der Mervenne

Joseph Nasch, 33 Avenue Montaigne

J. de Fleury (bookseller), 2 Rue Baste,
     19th arr.

Olga Ordinaire, 9 Rue Duranton, 15th arr.

Ariane Pathé, 3 Rue Quentin-Bauchart

Douglas Eyben

Anna Seidner

Marie Molitor

Pierrot 43 . . .

As we fumble through these efforts, certain names light up intermittently, like signals that might lead to a hidden path.

The name "Madame Hubersen," which I'd jotted down randomly, followed by a question mark, prompted merely a vague recollection at first. I tried to associate "Madame Hubersen"

with other names on my list. I hoped that between them and "Madame Hubersen," an illu-
minated line would appear, like the one on
the metro map that told you which route you
needed to take to get from Corvisart station to
Michel-Ange-Auteuil, or from Jasmin to Filles-
du-Calvaire. I had nearly reached the bottom
of the list and I felt like an amnesiac, trying to
break through a layer of ice and forgetfulness.
And then suddenly, I knew for certain that the
name "Madame Hubersen" was linked to that
of Madeleine Péraud. And that Madeleine Péraud had in fact taken Geneviève Dalame and
me, several times, to see that Madame Hubersen, who lived in an apartment on one of those
wide avenues in the western neighborhoods—
an avenue whose name I hesitate to write down
today, as if too precise a detail could still harm
me, nearly fifty years after the fact, and pro-
voke what they call "further investigation" into
a "case" in which I might have been implicated.

Perhaps I had wanted until now to erase that
Madame Hubersen from my memory, along

with other people I met back then, between the ages of seventeen and twenty-two.

But after half a century, the few people who witnessed your early years have finally disappeared—and anyway, it's doubtful that many of them would make the connection between what you've become and the vague image they've retained of a young man whose name they might not even recall.

My memory of Madame Hubersen is also rather vague. A brunette of about thirty with regular features and bobbed hair. She used to take us to dinner near her building, in one of those streets perpendicular to Avenue Foch— on the left side of the avenue, facing away from the Arc de Triomphe. And here I am, no longer afraid to provide topographical details. I tell myself that this is all so far in the past that it's covered by what the law calls amnesty. We would go on foot from her house to the restaurant that winter, a winter that was as harsh as the ones before it, next to which the winters of today seem rather mild; a winter like the ones I knew in the Haute-Savoie, when at night the air you breathed was frigid and clear and as intoxicating as ether. Madame Hubersen wore a fur coat of fairly classic cut. She had no doubt led a more bourgeois life than the one she was leading now, judging from the mess her apartment was in. It was on the top floor of a modern building, two or three rooms cluttered with paintings, African and Oceanic masks, Indian textiles.

About that Madame Hubersen, I know little apart from what Madeleine Péraud had told us, the first evening we went to visit her. She lived alone and was divorced from an American. She apparently knew a lot of people in ballet circles. One evening she had taken us a long distance, all the way to the Bassin de la Villette, to the home of a man who according to her threw a party, on the same date every year, in honor of the dancers. There, in a minuscule apartment, I had been amazed to see the ballet stars I so admired at the time, among them a young ballerina from the Opéra who later became a Carmelite nun. She is still alive today and is no doubt the only person who could tell me exactly who that mysterious dance lover was.

In my notebooks, I came across something I'd jotted down more than ten years ago, dated May 1, 2006: "The man with the Turkish name who, in the sixties, used to throw a party at his home for ballet dancers (Nureyev, Béjart, Babilée, Yvette Chauviré, etc.). He lived on one of the quays of the Bassin de la Villette or the Ourcq canal." And to make certain this memory was indeed real, I had checked the phone book for the man's name and address, since it's written down in blue ballpoint:

11 Quai de la Gironde (19th arrondissement)
Amram, R., COMbat 7314
Mouyal, Matathias, COMbat 8206 (1964
    directory)

That address and those two names are preceded by question marks, in the same blue ink.

I would see Madame Hubersen one last time, in the month of August 1967.

But before describing that encounter, I'd like to clarify something: I have occasionally run into the same people several times in the streets of Paris, people I didn't know. By dint of crossing paths with them, I grew to recognize their faces. I assumed they paid no attention to me and that only I had noticed these chance encounters; otherwise, we would have greeted each other or started a conversation. Most disturbing was when I kept running into the same person in different neighborhoods, in very separate parts

of town, as if fate—or chance—insisted on us
getting to know each other. And every time, I
felt remorse at letting that person go by without
saying anything. Many paths led away from that
crossing, and I had neglected one, perhaps the
best of all. As a consolation, I scrupulously re-
corded each of those fruitless encounters in my
notebook, specifying the exact spot and physi-
cal appearance of the anonymous party. Paris is
studded with nerve centers and the many forms
our lives might have taken.

Madame Hubersen, then: I ran into her one
last time that month of August, when I was living
in a tiny room in a clutch of buildings surrounding a small courtyard that opened onto Boulevard Gouvion-Saint-Cyr. It was very hot that
summer and the neighborhood was deserted.
You didn't even feel up to taking the metro in
search of a little activity nearer the center. You
let yourself be overcome by lassitude. The only
open restaurant on Boulevard Gouvion-Saint-
Cyr was called La Passée. I was afraid I wouldn't
be very welcome in that establishment. I imag-

ined a few shady customers sitting around a game of poker, but that night I decided to cross the threshold.

The décor in La Passée was like that of a country inn. A bar at the entrance and two rooms one after the other, the second looking out on a small garden. All at once, the sense of strangeness I felt in Paris in August got so bad that I wanted to double back and return as fast as possible to the sidewalk of Boulevard Gouvion-Saint-Cyr and the noise of the few automobiles heading toward Porte Maillot. But a woman led me to the second room and pointed me toward a table next to the garden.

I sat down with the feeling of being stuck in a dream, no doubt because I hadn't spoken to a soul in days. Never had the expression "cut off from the world" seemed so appropriate. No other customers, save for a woman on her own, seated at the back of the room. She was wearing a fur coat, which surprised me in the middle of August. She didn't seem to have noticed my presence. I recognized Madame Hubersen. She hadn't changed, and her fur coat was the same one she had worn three years earlier.

After a moment's hesitation, I walked over to her.

"Madame Hubersen?"

She raised her eyes to me, and didn't seem to recognize me.

"We met a few times three years ago . . . with Madeleine Péraud . . ."

She was still gaping at me, and I wondered whether she had heard.

"Oh yes . . . Of course . . ." she suddenly said, as if she'd suffered a momentary lapse. "With Madeleine Péraud . . . And have you had any news of Madeleine Péraud?"

I could see she was trying to bounce back. I had simply roused her too abruptly from a deep sleep.

"No, no news."

She gave me a sheepish smile. She was searching for her words.

"Do you remember?" I said to her. "You brought us to a party . . . with all those dancers . . ."

"Right . . . right . . . of course . . . I don't know if they still throw that party every year . . ."

It was as if she were alluding to some long-distant event, which was barely three years old but which for her belonged to another life. And I have to say that I had the same impression when I recalled all those guests sitting on the floor in the two rooms of that small apartment, and the full moon that winter night, above the Bassin de la Villette or the Ourcq canal.

"Are you still living at the same address?"

Maybe I had asked her that question to get a precise answer and not feel like I was dealing with a ghost.

"Still at the same address . . ."

She gave out a small laugh, for which I was grateful. She no longer seemed like a ghost.

"You ask such odd questions . . . And what about you — still at the same address?"

She seemed to be gently mocking me.

"Have a seat. Would you like to order something? I've already eaten . . ."

I sat down facing her. I intended to take my leave after a few moments, on the pretext of making a phone call. But once seated, I felt it would be difficult to stand up and cross the room to the exit. I was overcome by torpor.

"Don't mind the fur coat," she said. "I put it on tonight because I thought the temperature was about to drop. Apparently not."

But I didn't need any explanations. You have to take people as they are, with or without fur coats. If need be, ask a few discreet questions, gently, without arousing their suspicion, the better to understand them. And after all, I had met Madame Hubersen only three or four times and I never would have expected to run into her three years later. Encounters so brief they could easily have fallen into oblivion.

"So how do you know about this place?" I asked. "La Passée?"

"A friend of mine brought me here a few times. But he's away on holiday . . ."

She spoke in a clear, firm voice, and what she had just said made perfect sense. One often finds oneself alone in Paris in the month of August and in dubious places, in the image of that season when time seems to have stopped—places that disappear once life has regained its rhythm, and the city its normal appearance.

"You don't want anything to eat? How about something to drink?"

She picked up a carafe from the table and filled a large glass with what I thought was water, but whose taste surprised me when I'd taken a gulp: very strong alcohol. Then she poured some for herself. She swallowed not a gulp but half the glass, in one go, with a slight movement of her head.

"Aren't you drinking?" She seemed disappointed and a little embarrassed, as if I had cast her back into her solitude. So I emptied my glass as well.

"You see," she said, "we need to warm up despite the heat."

I felt she wanted to say something else, but was hesitating and couldn't find the words.

"I'll let you in on a little secret."

She laid her hand flat on mine to pluck up her courage.

"No matter how hot it gets, if you only knew how cold I am all the time . . ."

She gave me a look that was at once shy and questioning, waiting for an answer, or rather a reassuring diagnosis.

We left La Passée. She leaned on my arm along Boulevard Gouvion-Saint-Cyr. A breeze blew, the first in two weeks.

"Looks like you were right to wear your fur coat," I said.

She might have wanted to walk home. But in that case, we were heading in the wrong direction. I pointed this out to her.

"I feel like walking a bit, just to the first taxi stand."

At that late hour and in that season, there

was no traffic on Boulevard Gouvion-Saint-Cyr. It's strange, but in writing this today, I can hear the echo of our footsteps—or rather, of hers— on the empty sidewalk. We had arrived at the small courtyard where I lived. For a moment, I was tempted to take my leave, say that someone was waiting for me up in my room—a garret so small that at the door I had to fall onto the bed so as not to bump my head on the beam. And at the thought, I couldn't help laughing. She leaned more tightly against my arm.

"What's so funny?"

I didn't know what to answer. Was she really expecting one? With her free hand, she had raised the collar of her fur coat, as if the breeze had suddenly turned chilly.

"Do you still have those African and Oceanic masks in your apartment?" I asked her to break the silence.

She stopped and stared at me in surprise.

"You've got some memory!"

Yes, I do . . . But I also remember details of my life, people I've tried very hard to forget. I thought I had succeeded, and then out of the blue, after dozens of years, they rise to the surface like a drowned man, at a bend in the street, at certain hours of the day.

We were at Porte de Champerret. A lone taxi was waiting at the stand, in front of the group of buildings with brick façades.

"Will you come with me?" Madame Hubersen asked.

Once again, I almost told her someone was waiting in my room. But I suddenly felt bad about lying to her. So many lies already to run out on people, so many buildings with rear exits for quick escapes, so many appointments I didn't keep . . .

I climbed into the taxi with her. I thought the ride would be short, to her place, and that I could walk back.

"We're going to Versailles, Boulevard de la Reine," she told the driver.

I remained silent. I waited for an explanation.

"I'm afraid to go home. All those masks you

asked about before . . . They watch me, and mean me no good . . ."

She had said it in such a serious tone that I was left speechless. And then I found my voice again.

"I think you must be wrong. Those masks can't be as malevolent as all that . . ."

But I realized she wasn't joking. The taxi had turned onto Boulevard Gouvion-Saint-Cyr, in the direction opposite the one we'd been following earlier. We had nearly reached the little courtyard where my building was.

"I have to go home now," I said. "It's just up here, on the right . . ."

"Be nice and come with me to Versailles."

Her request was not to be denied, as if it were a moral imperative. The taxi had stopped at a red light in front of the large fire station. I was tempted to push open the door, mumble a polite excuse, and take my leave. But I told myself I had plenty of time for that on the way to Versailles. I thought about that book I'd read, *Dreams and How to Direct Them,* which says that you can interrupt dreams at any moment, and even make them change course. All I had to do was concentrate a little for the taxi driver to let us off in front of Madame Hubersen's building, and to forget we were going to Versailles. Madame Hubersen too.

"Are you sure you don't want to go home?" I asked her quietly.

She moved her face close to mine and said, also quietly:

"You have no idea what it's like to come home to that apartment every evening . . . and be there alone with those masks . . . And besides, for a while now I've been afraid to take the elevator . . ."

I was still too young to know the anxiety she felt when returning home alone. Personally, I had no problem taking the elevator, then climbing the small stairway and following the hallway that led to that garret where I couldn't even stand upright. And now that I'm nearly forty years older than Madame Hubersen was at the time, I tell myself it was strange at her age to let herself be prey to such anxiety. But perhaps we shouldn't put too much stock in certain notions, like "the insouciance of youth."

We stopped at another red light, near the restaurant La Passée. There were other stoplights along the way—I told myself—that would allow me to escape. It wouldn't be the first time: twice before, I had bolted from a car that was bringing me back to boarding school on Sunday evening; and again, at around twenty, when I found myself in the company of several individuals in a Chevrolet whose driver was drunk. As luck would have it, I had been sitting by the door.

"You really don't want to go back home?" I asked Madame Hubersen again.

"Not right now. Tomorrow, when it's light out."

We had arrived at the edge of the Bois de Boulogne, and Madame Hubersen had closed her eyes. I checked that the door wasn't locked from inside, as was sometimes the case in taxis at night. No. I still had a little time to make up my mind.

At Porte d'Auteuil, Madame Hubersen's head rolled onto my shoulder. She had fallen asleep. If I left the car now, I would have to do it gently, by sliding quietly over the seat and not slamming the door. Her head, so light on my shoulder, was like a mark of trust on her part, and I had qualms about betraying that trust. Porte de Saint-Cloud. We were about to cross the Seine, enter the tunnel, then take the western highway. And there would be no more red lights.

From the age of eleven, escapes played a large part in my life. Escapes from boarding schools; escapes from Paris on a night train when I was supposed to show up at the Reuilly barracks for my military service; appointments that I disappointed; or stock phrases to get away: "Wait here, I just have to go buy cigarettes," and that promise I must have made dozens and dozens of times, not keeping it once: "I'll be right back."

Today, I feel some regret about it. Although I'm not very good at introspection, I would like to understand why flight was my modus operandi.

And it lasted a fairly long time, I'd say until the age of twenty-two. Was it like those childhood illnesses that have such peculiar names: whooping cough, chicken pox, scarlet fever? Beyond my personal case, I've always dreamed of writing a treatise on escape, in the manner of those French moralists and memorialists whose style I've so admired since I was an adolescent: Cardinal de Retz, La Bruyère, La Rochefoucauld, Vauvenargues . . . But I can only relate concrete details, precise places and moments. In particular, that afternoon in the summer of '65 when I found myself at the bar of a narrow café at the beginning of Boulevard Saint-Michel, which stood out from the other cafés in the neighborhood in that it didn't cater to students. A long counter, like the ones in Pigalle or around Saint-Lazare train station. I realized, that afternoon, that I had been letting myself drift and that, if I didn't do something about it immediately, I'd be swept away. I had always thought I was in no danger, that I enjoyed a kind of immunity in my capacity as a nocturnal spectator—as one eighteenth-century writer who explored the mysteries of nighttime Paris had styled himself. But in this case, my curiosity had led me a bit too far. I felt what they call the "wind of the cannonball." I had to disappear right away if I wanted to stay out of trouble. This would be a much bigger escape than the others. I had hit bottom, and my only recourse was to push off hard with my heel to rise back to the surface.

The evening before, an event had occurred that I alluded to twenty years later, in 1985, in a chapter of a novel. It was a way of ridding myself of a weight, of setting down in black and white a kind of partial confession. But twenty years was too short a time for certain witnesses to disappear, and I wondered what the statute of limitations was before the law would give up pursuing the perpetrators or their accomplices and drape them once and for all in a veil of amnesty and oblivion.

The person I had met several weeks earlier, whose name I hesitate to write—even after fifty years, I'm wary of precise details that would allow someone to identify her—had called me very late one night, in that month of June 1965, to tell me there had been an "accident" in the apartment of Martine Hayward, 2 Avenue Rodin, where we had been introduced, and where, every Sunday evening, the motley group that Martine Hayward called "the nighthawks" would gather. She begged me to come.

In the living room of the apartment, on the carpet, lay the body of Ludo F., the shadiest member of that group of "nighthawks." She had killed him "by accident," she told me, while holding a gun that she had "found on one of the bookshelves in the library." She handed me the weapon, which she had put back in its suede case. But what was she doing alone in the apartment that evening with Ludo F.? She would explain everything "as soon as we're far away from here, in the open air."

Without switching on the hall light, I took her arm and helped her down the stairs in the dark, preferring not to take the elevator. On the ground floor, light behind the glassed door of the concierge's lodge. I pulled her toward the street exit and, just as we passed by the lodge, a man came out, small and dark with a brush-cut. He watched us in the dim light as I groped at the street door. It was locked. After a moment—and that moment seemed an eternity—I spotted the button on the wall that released the latch. I heard the click and pulled it open. I performed each movement in slow motion, to make it as precise as possible, and I didn't take my eyes off the short man with brush-cut hair, as if I were daring him to etch my features in his memory. She grew impatient, and I let her go ahead of me; then, before following her out, I stood still for a few moments in the doorway, my eyes riveted on the concierge. I expected him to come toward me, but he too stood still, watching. Time had stopped. She was about a dozen yards ahead of me and I didn't know if I could catch up: my steps grew slower, ever slower, and I felt as if I were floating, my slightest movements broken down.

We arrived at Place du Trocadéro. About two in the morning. The cafés were closed. I felt increasingly calm and I breathed more and more normally, without having to make an effort. Where did such tranquility come from? From the silence and limpid air of Place du Trocadéro? That air felt as soft and glacial as on the slopes of the Haute-Savoie. I was certainly under the sway of the book I had been reading the past several days, *Dreams and How to Direct Them* by Hervey de Saint-Denys, which lay on my bedside table. I felt like I had communicated my calm to her and that she and I were now walking in step. She asked where we were going, exactly. It was much too late to return to Montmartre, to the Hôtel Alsina, or to her place in Saint-Maur-des-Fossés. I spotted a hotel sign at the very beginning of one of the avenues that led away from Place du Trocadéro. But I had kept the revolver in its suede case in one of my jacket pockets. I looked for a sewer in which to drop it. Since I was holding it in my hand, she threw me some worried looks. I tried to reassure her. We were alone in the plaza. And even if, by chance, someone was watching us from a dark window in one of the buildings, it didn't matter. He couldn't do anything to us. I had only to redirect the dream, following Hervey de Saint-Denys's prescriptions, like giving the steering wheel a slight turn. And the car would roll smoothly— one of those American cars from the period, that seemed to glide over the water, in silence.

We skirted the plaza and I ended up shoving the gun in the bottom of a trash can, in front of the maritime museum. Then we turned down the avenue with the small hotel whose sign I had spotted. Hôtel Malakoff. Since then, I've had occasion to walk past it and, one evening five years ago, when it was as warm as on that night in June 1965, I stopped at the entrance, thinking I might take a room, perhaps the same one as back then. It would serve as a pretext, I told myself, to flip through the registration cards and see whether my name was still there for the date of June 28, 1965. But did they keep the old registers, which might be checked from time to time by members of the vice squad? That night fifty years ago, given the late hour, only the night watchman was on duty at the reception desk. She stood back, and I was the one who wrote my name, address, and date of birth on the registration card, even though the watchman didn't ask us for anything, not even an ID. I was sure that Hervey de Saint-Denys, who was so familiar with dreams and how to redirect them, would have approved of my compunction. As I traced the letters—and I wanted to use my best handwriting, with proper upstrokes and downstrokes, but the ballpoint pen didn't allow it—I felt a soothing calm that I had never experienced before. I even put down my address as 2 Avenue Rodin, where Ludo F. lay stretched out on the carpet, resting in peace.

In the days that followed, the anxiety that had gripped me in that bar on Boulevard Saint-Michel died down. Perhaps it had been caused by the proximity of the courthouse and the police headquarters, which were visible nearby, just across the bridge. I knew that detectives frequented certain cafés in Place Saint-Michel. From then on, we remained in Montmartre; we felt safer there, and ended up wondering whether the events of the other night had really happened.

I have some trepidation about bringing up those days. They are the last and most memorable days of a part of my youth. From then on, nothing would have quite the same coloration. Did the death of Ludo F., a man we barely knew, serve as a slap of reality? Still later after that event, I was often jolted awake by gunshots and, after a moment, I realized those gunshots hadn't been fired in real life, but in my dreams. Every day, upon leaving the Hôtel Alsina, I went to buy the newspapers in a small shop on Rue Caulaincourt—*France-Soir*, *L'Aurore*, the ones that carried human interest stories—and read them in secret, so as not to alarm her. Nothing about Ludo F. Evidently he was of no interest to anyone. Or else the people in his circle had managed to cover up his death. No doubt to avoid getting mixed up in it themselves. A little farther up Rue Caulaincourt, at the sidewalk of the café Le Rêve, I wrote in the margins of one of those newspapers the names of the people I remembered from those Sunday evening "gatherings," where I had met her.

And today, fifty years later, I can't help, once more, writing on this blank sheet some of those names. Martine and Philippe Hayward, Jean Terrail, Andrée Karvé, Guy Lavigne, Roger Favart and his wife, who had freckles and gray eyes . . . others . . .

Not one of them has been in touch these last fifty years. I must have been invisible to them at the time. Or else, quite simply, we live at the mercy of certain silences.

June. July 1965. The days passed, that summer in Montmartre, all of them the same, with their late mornings and sunny afternoons. You had only to let yourself glide into their tranquil current and float on your back. We would end up forgetting all about the dead man, about whom she didn't seem to know much, except that she had met him when she worked in a perfume shop on Rue de Ponthieu. He had come in to talk to her, and she had run into him again in the café next door, where she usually ordered a sandwich for lunch. A few times, he had brought her to those Sunday evening gatherings that Martine Hayward hosted on Avenue Rodin, where she and I had met. That was all of it. And what had happened there, the other night, was an "accident." And she would say no more about it.

When I think about that summer, it feels as though it's become detached from the rest of my life. A parenthesis, or rather, an ellipsis.

Several years after that, I was living in Montmartre, at 9 Rue de l'Orient, with the woman I loved. The neighborhood was not the same. Neither was I. We had both regained our innocence. One afternoon, I stopped in front of the Hôtel Alsina, which had been broken up into apartments. The Montmartre of summer 1965, as I thought I envisioned it in memory, suddenly seemed to me an imaginary Montmartre. And I no longer had anything to fear.

W e rarely crossed the southernmost boundary, defined by the median strip of Boulevard de Clichy. We kept to a fairly narrow sector, through which rose Rue Caulaincourt. That month of July, we were the only ones at the sidewalk tables of Le Rêve; and in the afternoons, a bit farther north, we were also alone in the half-light of the San Cristobal, halfway up the stairway at the Lamarck-Caulaincourt metro stop. Our actions were always the same, in the same places, at the same hours, and under the same sun. I remember empty streets on sweltering days. And yet, a menace hung in the air. The body on the carpet, in the apartment that we had left without turning off the lamps . . . The windows would remain lit in broad daylight, like an alarm signal. I tried to understand why I had stood there so long, motionless in the presence of the concierge. And what a strange idea to have written, on the registration card at the Hôtel Malakoff, my name and the address of the apartment, 2 Avenue Rodin . . . They'd notice that a "homicide" had been committed that same night at that same address. What kind of vertigo had come over me as I was filling out the card? Or was it that the book by Hervey de Saint-Denys, which I'd been reading when she called and begged me to come, had muddled my thoughts? I was convinced it was all a bad dream. I was in no danger. I could "direct" that dream as I pleased and, if I so desired, could wake myself up at any moment.

Early one afternoon, we were walking up the slope of Rue Caulaincourt, empty in the sunlight, and it felt as if we were the only inhabitants of Montmartre. I told her, to reassure myself, that

we were in a little port on the Mediterranean at
siesta time. Nobody at the San Cristobal. We sat
down at a table near the tinted windows that left
the room in semidarkness. It was cool, like at
the bottom of an aquarium. "It's a bad dream.
Just a bad dream . . ." I hardly realized I was
saying this aloud. The body of Ludo F. on the
carpet and the lights we left on in the apartment . . . She laid her hand on mine. "Don't
think about it," she said in a murmur. Until that
moment, I'd been under the impression that *she*
didn't want to think about it, and in the early
days I didn't dare tell her I read the newspapers
every morning, dreading to find a notice with
Ludo F.'s name printed in it. But she shared my
fears. We didn't need to say it to each other, we
had only to exchange a glance. The evening, for
instance, when we came home to Avenue Junot,
to the Hôtel Alsina, as we were taking the elevator. It was an elevator in light-colored wood
with two glassed swinging doors, as they still had
back then. It rose so slowly that it threatened to
stop between floors. I was afraid a policeman

would be waiting for us at the door to our room, while another had taken up position downstairs, at the reception desk. They were the same ones who frequented the cafés on Place Saint-Michel. I had been able to identify them by overhearing bits of their conversations. I was the one they were after, since they knew my name. She had nothing to worry about. I wanted to tell her this, right there in the elevator, but we had arrived at our floor. No one at the door. Or in the room. It would be for another time. Once again I had managed, at the last moment, to redirect the dream, following the prescriptions of Hervey de Saint-Denys.

There were two restaurants we went to in the evening: one on the corner of Rue Constance and Rue Joseph-de-Maistre, the other at the end of Rue Caulaincourt, at the foot of the stairway. There were a lot of people in both, which contrasted with the empty streets in daytime. We passed unnoticed amid those crowds, and the hubbub of their conversations protected us. Customers came in until midnight, and they set up tables on the sidewalk. We stayed as late as possible, among all those diners who seemed like holiday-makers. After all, we too were on holiday. At around one

in the morning, when it was time to return to
the Hôtel Alsina, our eyes met. We would have
to walk up deserted Avenue Junot and enter the
hotel without knowing who might be at the reception desk. At that hour, we avoided taking
the elevator. We didn't feel very reassured at
first, standing in the silence of the room. I stayed
behind the door, listening for the sound of footsteps in the hallway. In short, it was when there
were a lot of people around, in the evening, in
the two restaurants, that we felt most at ease,
like just two more vacationers who had spent the
day on the beach at Pampelonne. We could even
talk about the delicate subject that preoccu-
pied us both. Our voices were lost in the din of
other voices, and we carefully avoided precise
terms, merely alluded to things, so that those at
the next table wouldn't understand even if they
were eavesdropping. We left out certain words,
spoke in ellipses. I would have liked her to give
me further information about Ludo F., for I was
sure she knew more about him than she let on.
That first meeting in the perfume shop on Rue

de Ponthieu did not seem entirely consistent with the truth. Some details had been left out, I was sure of it. But I could sense her reluctance to answer. What worried me was that they might establish a connection between her and the one we called "the dead man." Was there any tangible proof that she had known "the dead man"? A letter? Her name and address in his little black book? What would the others say if they were interrogated about her and her relations with "the dead man"? To each of my questions, she merely shrugged. She didn't seem on very close terms with the others who attended the Sunday evening gatherings at 2 Avenue Rodin, at Martine Hayward's. Whenever I mentioned a name— Andrée Karvé, Guy Lavigne, Roger Favart and his wife, Vincent Berlen, Marion Le Phat-Vinh, those few names I had scribbled in the margins of a newspaper and that I wrest one final time from oblivion—she shook her head. Besides, she said, none of those people knew anything about her and couldn't testify against her. She leaned toward me as if she wanted to add something under her breath, but it was a needless precaution: our neighbors were talking loudly and, at that same instant, the voice of the guitarist who came by the restaurant on Rue Caulaincourt at the same time each evening to play a Neapolitan song by Roberto Murolo, "Anema e core," added to the noise of the conversations. She whispered, "You shouldn't have used your real name on the hotel register."

I'm trying to recall my state of mind at that moment. The next day, alone in the bar on Boulevard Saint-Michel, I had been gripped by panic, but it hadn't lasted long. After hitting bottom, I rebounded to the surface. I told myself: This will be the start of a new life for me. And the one I had lived up until then seemed like a tangled dream from which I had just awoken. I suddenly understood the meaning of the expression "the future lies before you." Yes, I ended up convincing myself that, from the vantage point of the future, I had nothing more to fear, and that from then on I was inoculated by a vaccine or protected by a diplomatic passport.

"I'm not in danger anymore," I told her. "Not anymore." And my tone must have been so emphatic that the diner closest to us, a blond of about forty, who could easily have been one of the detectives I had spotted in the cafés on Place Saint-Michel, looked over at me. I held his gaze and smiled.

One afternoon, she wanted to go collect some "things" at her place, in Saint-Maur. It was the only day that summer on which we left Montmartre. We waited for the train on the platform at Bastille.

"You don't think it's too dangerous to go there, do you?" she asked. "They might have found my address."

At that moment, I was feeling no particular concern.

"They haven't identified you. They couldn't possibly have the address of an unknown person."

She nodded, as if what I had just said struck her as an incontrovertible truth. She repeated the word "unknown" several times, as if to persuade herself that she was out of danger and that she would forever remain an unknown person.

We were alone in the train compartment. A weekday, an off-peak hour of the afternoon, in midsummer. The night we had met in Martine Hayward's apartment, we had walked at around two in the morning up to Place de l'Alma. She had hailed a taxi to go back to Saint-Maur, and she had made a date to see me there the next day, writing her address on a scrap of paper: 35 Avenue du Nord. And the next day, I had found myself on the same train, at the same hour of the afternoon, along the same route as now: Bastille. Saint-Mandé. Bois de Vincennes. Nogent-sur-Marne. Saint-Maur.

We followed Avenue du Nord, lined with trees whose branches formed a vault. It was empty that afternoon, like the streets of Montmartre. Dapples of sunlight and shadows of the branches on the sidewalk and pavement. The first time I'd come here, two weeks earlier, she had been waiting for me in front of her house. We had walked all the way to La Varenne-Saint-Hilaire and the sidewalk tables of a hotel on the banks of the Marne, called the Petit Ritz.

This time, she hesitated a moment before opening the street door and threw me a worried glance. She was feeling the same momentary apprehension as had seized us that night in Montmartre, when we returned to the Hôtel Alsina. A neglected lawn. Grass had invaded the path that sloped down to the door of the house. The lawn formed a kind of valley and the house rose from it partway down the hill, so that at first it was hard to distinguish the ground floor. This house occupied a precarious position and seemed at the mercy of a landslide. It looked like a cross between a private cottage and a suburban two-story.

She told me to wait downstairs while she got her things together. A large room. The only piece of furniture was a couch. The windows looked out, to one side, on the sloping lawn that blocked the horizon, and to the other, on a kind of waste ground at the bottom of that slope. It really gave the sense that the house was in a delicate balance and that it might tip over at any moment. And besides, the silence was so complete that after fifteen minutes I was afraid she had run out on me—just as I myself had often done with the words, "Wait here, I'll be right back," when walking past a building with a rear exit, like the one on Place Saint-Michel where you could escape via Rue de l'Hirondelle, or at 1 Rue Lord-Byron, which led you through a maze of hallways and elevators to Avenue des Champs-Elysées.

She reappeared just when I was sure she had vanished and was about to go upstairs to see for myself. She was carrying a black leather suitcase. She sat down next to me on the couch. And all of a sudden, I felt the same thought cross our minds: the body of Ludo F. in the apartment on Avenue Rodin.

* * *

I had taken her suitcase, which was rather heavy, and again we followed Avenue du Nord. She was relieved to have left the house behind. So was I. There are certain places that don't arouse your suspicions at first because they look so normal, but after a few moments they give off a bad aura. And I had always been sensitive to what they call "the spirit of the place." So much so that I left very quickly if I felt the slightest doubt, like that winter afternoon in the café La Source when I was with Geneviève Dalame's brother and his friend with the face of a former stable boy. Moreover, I tried to probe the matter by listing in my notebooks the exact places and addresses where I'd decided not to linger. It's a special gift, a sixth sense that you find, for instance, in truffle hounds, and that is also reminiscent of certain devices, like mine detectors. Over the following years, I saw that I hadn't been mistaken about most of those places and addresses. I learned why they gave off a bad aura, often twenty or thirty years after the fact, from random comments, coincidences, old newspaper clippings. Sometimes all it took was a few words of conversation overheard in a café.

Now and again I paused on Avenue du Nord to set her suitcase down on the sidewalk. It was one heavy piece of luggage. I finally asked if she'd stuffed Ludo F.'s body in there. She remained expressionless, but didn't appear to appreciate the joke. Was it a joke? Sometimes, in my dreams, and even at the very moment I'm writing this, I can feel in my right hand the weight of that suitcase, like a healed wound that still aches in winter or on rainy days. An old regret? It pursued me, without my being able to identify its cause. One time, I had an intuition that the cause dated from before my birth, and that this regret had spread along a safety fuse. My intuition was so fleeting, a match whose tiny flame flares for a few seconds in the dark before going out . . .

It was still a long road to La Varenne station, where I had arrived from Paris on the day of our first date. I proposed we spend that evening and night at the Petit Ritz, as we had done two weeks earlier. But she reminded me that I had signed the register of the Petit Ritz with my real name, as I had done recently at the Hôtel Malakoff. And besides, the regulars at the Petit Ritz knew her by sight. Better to lie low.

I wonder if it was the dim and distant memory of a summer afternoon spent in Saint-Maur that caused me to write these few lines in a notebook forty-six years later, on December 26, 2011:

"Dream. I'm with a police superintendent who hands me a summons on yellowed paper. The first sentence mentions a crime about which I have to testify. I don't want to read these pages. I misplace them. Later, I learn that it concerns a girl from Saint-Maur-des-Fossés who killed a man older than she in Marly-le-Roi (?). I don't know what I've been witness to.

"This corresponds to a recurring dream: they have already arrested certain individuals but haven't identified me. And I live under threat of being arrested in turn once they realize I have connections with the 'guilty parties.' But guilty of what?"

L ast year, at the bottom of a large envelope, among expired navy blue passports and report cards from a children's home and a boarding school in the Haute-Savoie, I came upon some typed sheets.

At first, I hesitated to reread those few pages of onionskin held together by a rusty paperclip. I wanted to get rid of them right away, but that struck me as impossible, like radioactive waste that it's no use burying hundreds of feet underground.

The only way to defuse this thin file once

and for all was to copy out portions of it and blend them into the pages of a novel, as I did thirty years ago. That way, no one would know whether they belonged to reality or the realm of dreams. Today, March 10, 2017, I again opened the pale green sleeve, removed the paperclip that left rust stains on the first sheet and, before ripping the whole thing to shreds and leaving not a single material trace, I'll copy over a few sentences and then be done with it.

On the first sheet, June 29, 1965

Criminal Investigations Division. Vice Squad.

Location of the slugs.

Three slugs were found, corresponding to the three spent shells . . .

Regarding the various hypotheses about what led to the murder of Ludovic F. . . .

On the second sheet, July 5, 1965

Criminal Investigations Division. Vice Squad.

The alleged Ludovic F. had used this alias

for about twenty years. He is actually a certain Aksel B., aka Bowels. Born Feb. 20, 1916, in Frederiksberg, Denmark. No known profession. At large since April 1949, having resided in Paris (16th arr.). Last known domicile: 48 Rue des Belles-Feuilles.

On the fourth sheet, July 5, 1965

Note

Criminal Investigations Division

Vice Squad.

Jean D.

Born July 25, 1945, in Boulogne-Billancourt (Seine) . . . Two hotel registration cards have been found in the name of Jean D., who filled them out in June:

June 7, 1965: Hotel-restaurant Petit Ritz, 68 Avenue du 11-Novembre in La Varenne-Saint-Hilaire (Seine-et-Marne).

June 28, 1965: Hôtel Malakoff, 3 Avenue Raymond-Poincaré, Paris 16, on which he indicated his home address as 2 Avenue Rodin (16th).

At both the Petit Ritz and the Malakoff, he was accompanied by a young woman of about twenty,

average height, brown hair, blue eyes, whose de-
scription matches the deposition of Mr. R., concierge, 2 Avenue Rodin, Paris 16.

So far, this young woman has not been
identified.

Although she was never identified, I tracked her down twenty years later. Her name was in the Paris phone book for that year, a first and last name that could only be hers. 76 Boulevard Sérurier, 19th arrondissement. 208-7668.

It was in the month of August. The telephone didn't answer. Several times, in late afternoon, I stood watch in front of the brick building behind which stretches the park called Butte-du-Chapeau-Rouge. I didn't know this neighborhood. It's other people who reveal to you a city's most secret and distant areas, by making appointments at such-and-such an address. When they disappear, they drag you in their wake. In late afternoon, at the bottom of Boulevard Sérurier, it felt as though time had stopped. The sunlight and silence, the blue of the sky, the ochre color of the building, the green trees in the park . . . all of this formed a contrast, in my memory, with the Bassin de la Villette or the Ourcq canal, a bit farther north in the same arrondissement, which I had discovered one December night thanks to Madame Hubersen.

Nothing had changed for me. That summer, I waited at the doorway of a building, as I had waited on the sidewalk, twenty-five years earlier, in winter, for Stioppa's daughter. If anyone had asked me what was the point of all this, I think I would have answered simply, "I'm trying to solve the mysteries of Paris."

One afternoon that late August, I recognized her silhouette from afar, at the top of Boulevard Sérurier. I wasn't surprised. All you need is a little patience. I remembered my bedside reading back when we'd known each other: *Eter-*

nity by the Stars and *The Eternal Return of the Same*
. . . She was walking down the slope, a suitcase
in her hand, but not the black leather one I'd
carried to La Varenne station. A tin suitcase. It
reflected the sunlight. I joined her halfway down
Boulevard Sérurier.

I took her suitcase. We didn't need to speak.
We had left on foot from Saint-Maur, 35 Avenue du Nord, and it had taken us twenty years
to reach 76 Boulevard Sérurier. This suitcase
seemed much lighter than the other one. So
light that I wondered whether it was empty. No
doubt, as the years pass, you end up shedding
all the weights you dragged behind you, and all
the regrets.

I noticed a scar across her forehead. A car
accident, she said. One of those accidents that
make you lose your memory. And yet she had
recognized me. But she didn't seem to remember the events of summer 1965.

She was just back from the South and asked
me to walk her home. We could have strolled in

the middle of the boulevard that afternoon, for it was deserted, like the streets of Montmartre in the past, at the same hour and in the same season. And for me, those two summers blend together.

Between the pages of a novel, I came across a leaf from a datebook bearing the date Wednesday, April 20, and the mention "Saint Odette," but without giving the year. The novel is called *Tempo di Roma*, and it seems to me I read it toward the end of the sixties. At the time, I must have used the leaf as a bookmark. Or else I had bought the novel secondhand on the quays and the leaf was already in it. Written on the leaf were some directions in ink, in the color called "aqua blue":

Southern Highway or Route 7
Or Gare de Lyon
Nemours. Moret
Exit at Nemours
Leave Nemours to the right
Sens road for 10 km
Turn right
Remauville
Last house in the village, to the right facing
    the church
Green door
525-6631
432-5601

The two phone numbers no longer worked. Each time I dialed them, I heard very distant voices calling to each other, or pursuing a conversation of which you couldn't make out a single word. I believe those voices belonged to the mysterious "network" of people who used to take advantage of the vacancy left by disconnected phone lines to communicate with each other.

The irregular handwriting in blue ink might have been mine, but if so, I must have jotted down those directions in haste, from the rushed instructions of someone who barely had time to give them, or who said them in a low voice so as not to attract attention.

I'd been wanting to get to the bottom of this for several months, but I kept putting off my plan of going to the premises. And besides, those premises must have changed, or disappeared, or become inaccessible if you didn't have an old Geological Survey map.

Today I've made up my mind, I'm going to follow those directions right to the end. Over these past months, I wondered whether I hadn't already done so in the past, for the name "Nemours" rang a bell. Perhaps I hadn't continued past Nemours. Or else a double of myself had gone to the last house in the village and the green door. A double or doppelganger of those mentioned in *Eternity by the Stars,* one of my bedside books. Thousands and thousands of doubles of yourself follow the thousands of paths that you didn't take at various crossroads in your life, because you thought there was but a single one.

Among the old Geological Survey maps I'd bought nearly fifty years ago, I found the one for Nemours and environs. It indicates roads, paths, and villages that no longer appear on the current Michelin map for that region. I would have to follow the earlier map if I wanted to reach my destination.

I preferred to leave at around five in the afternoon. It was the beginning of September and the sun was still setting late. So as not to risk getting lost, I supplemented the itinerary on the datebook page, consulting the old Geological Survey map. I planned a few detours, the better to learn the terrain and thus explore some alternate routes.

Nemours. Moret
Go through Veneux-les-Sablons (Rte. 6)
After Moret, take the Orvanne valley
Cross through Lorrez-le-Boccage
 (Rte. D-218)

Villecerf (D-218)

Dormelles

Then head back toward Nemours

Leave Nemours to the right

Go through Laversanne

Sens road for 10 km

Cut through Bazoches-sur-le-Betz and
    the Baslins farm

Return via Egreville and Chaintreaux

Remauville

Last house in the village, to the right,
    facing the church

Vieux Lavoir slope to the green door

Alley. Sleeping Beauty castle

My handwriting was much steadier than the blue ink on the datebook leaf. The more precise I made the directions, the more it was as if I had already followed them, and I no longer needed to consult the old Geological Survey map. But was it really the right way? In our memories blend images of roads that we have taken, and we can't recall what regions they cross.

Patrick Modiano, winner of the 2014 Nobel Prize in Literature, was born in Boulogne-Billancourt, France, in 1945, and published his first novel, *La Place de l'Etoile*, in 1968. In 1978, he was awarded the Prix Goncourt for *Rue des Boutiques Obscures* (published in English as *Missing Person*), and in 1996 he received the Grand Prix National des Lettres for his body of work. Modiano's other writings in English translation include *Suspended Sentences, Pedigree: A Memoir, After the Circus, Paris Nocturne, Little Jewel, Sundays in August,* and *Such Fine Boys* (all published by Yale University Press), as well as the memoir *Dora Bruder,* the screenplay *Lacombe, Lucien,* and the novels *So You Don't Get Lost in the Neighborhood, Young Once, In the Café of Lost Youth,* and *The Black Notebook.*

Mark Polizzotti has translated more than fifty books from the French, including works by Gustave Flaubert, Marguerite Duras, Jean Echenoz, Raymond Roussel, and seven other volumes by Patrick Modiano. A Chevalier of the Ordre des Arts et des Lettres and the recipient of a 2016 American Academy of Arts and Letters Award for Literature, he is the author of eleven books, including *Revolution of the Mind: The Life of André Breton,* which was a finalist for the PEN/Martha Albrand Award for First Nonfiction; *Luis Buñuel's Los Olvidados; Bob Dylan: Highway 61 Revisited;* and *Sympathy for the Traitor: A Translation Manifesto.* He directs the publications program at The Metropolitan Museum of Art in New York.